Contents:

This book of short stories has been inspired by my recent trip to Florida. I love the place it is so friendly and open.
I was very fortunate to be over there for the Halloween celebrations with Universal Studios, Busch Gardens and the American people themselves.
An experience to enjoy, scare and I look forward to being there again next year.......

A Whistling In the Trees

I sit here on my own, in the dark, listening.

Listening to the whistling of the wind in the trees, listening as it gathers momentum and voice. I know that ***IT*** is coming for me. The thing that should have stayed dead and buried in hell, where it belonged, I didn't know that we had woken it until it was too late, much too late.

It had all started on the night that a few of us had decided to try a Ouija board session. What started as a bit of fun was now ending terribly. Two of my friends were dead, half eaten the police had said when they had found the bodies. I don't know what is going on all I do know is the sense of foreboding I feel as I sit listening to the whistling in the trees and knowing it is my turn to learn of the power we unleashed. I have felt this feeling before on the night of the Ouija, a strange feeling I had on the way home, the night that has been wiped from my memory.

It had been a Friday night like any other really, just a few friends gathering for a drink at the local pub and then back to either one of ours to finish the night off with a take away and a few more drinks. This time it had been Adrian's turn to host the after- hours party, little did we know what he had in store for the five of us that night.

When we were all burdened with our goodies we made our way back to his flat and were greeted with a table in the middle of the room surrounded by chairs and two large candle sticks perched on top of the table. As we all moved in closer we saw that in the middle of the table was a Ouija board and a glass resting in the middle of it. Next to that was a pad and pencil, obviously for jotting down what the lettering spelled out.

At that moment a cold chill travelled up my spine, but I didn't want to be the one called a party pooper. Everyone excitedly took their places round the table and began to eat and drink. Once we were all finished and plates were dispatched to the kitchen and glasses replenished, Adrian explained to us the workings of the Ouija. Or at least he tried to in his slurred, drunken voice until a couple of people told him to shut up, sit down and get on with it.

The candles were lit and we all sat round the table with one finger only from each of us touching the glass lightly. We were told that under no circumstances were we to push on the glass, just let it glide over the board and do its work.

A terrible silence came over the room and as the candles flickered I could have sworn I could smell sulphur. Probably a little bit of extra show care of Adrian, so I had thought.

We had all sat there for what seemed an age with Adrian asking questions and nothing happened. We laughed and took our fingers off the glass and it now started to move.

Adrian began to write furiously following the lettering as the glass moved quickly from one letter to the other.

When it stopped, Adrian looked up from the pad and read "Beware the Moon". That was it all of it.

Mary, Adrian's partner started to laugh, whether it was the drink or just nerves of what had just happened. Suddenly and violently, the glass shot off the table and crashed against the wall and the room went so icy cold that our breath was visible. She stopped laughing and suddenly muttered whispers came from the other two guests, making excuses to make their way back home, grabbing coats, and hurrying out into the night then there was just Adrian, Mary and myself left. My eyes took a while to adjust when the lights were flicked back on suddenly and the candles blown out. There is was again, the smell of sulphur stronger than before. It must have been the candles all along, I remembered thinking to myself.

Mary had shuffled off into the kitchen and returned with a dust pan and brush to sweep up the smashed glass. I watched her nervously making sure she had every last shard of glass swept up before disappearing once more and then coming back in with the Hoover, just to make sure. Adrian had offered me another drink but I had excused myself by telling him I best get home as it was getting late. He told me he would drive me until I reminded him how much he had drunk this evening and after turning down him calling a cab, I left and promised to call them tomorrow. As the door shut and I found myself on the doorstep, I could still hear the droning of the Hoover coming from inside the house. Up in the sky was the biggest and brightest of full moons I had ever seen. I shivered and pulled my coat tightly about me and made my way home.

I don't know really how I got home, but know that I woke up at 7am in bed and not in my clothes, for once. That was sometimes the way of it when I had been drinking the night before, I would wake up in the clothes I had been in the night before. But not this morning and as I lifted myself up on my elbows, I could just make out a pile of clothes at the end of the bed. Sinking back down into the pillows, it suddenly hit me what had happened last night. Probably some trick played by Adrian, he was always known as a prankster, but Mary had been terrified when the glass had smashed. Maybe he had set her up too. I pushed myself up out of bed and headed for a shower.

Once that was all done, I made myself some coffee and switched on the news. I just caught the tail end of a police appeal and a phone number and made a mental not that I would have a look online later to see what that was about. Thank god it was Saturday, a good lounge around, do some work on the computer I needed to catch up on before Monday then I would call Mary & Adrian to see if they fancied going for lunch.

I had busied myself in computer work until two

o'clock and when I finally shut the computer off I had forgotten about the news I wanted to catch up on, that was until I called Adrian. He asked me as soon as I called if I had seen the news I told him I had not. It was then he told me that the two friends of his that had left rather quickly last night had been found dead, but not only that it looked as though someone had half eaten them and they were appealing for witnesses to the last known whereabouts of the couple. Adrian asked me if I had seen them on the way home and I had told him I had seen no one, which was true because I could not remember anything from leaving there last night. He told me he had already called the police and told them when they were with us and when they left, but he had not told the police about the Ouija session as he felt this to be irrelevant to what had happened to them. Was he worried that they would laugh at him, heaven knows but I decided when it was my turn I would not reveal this information either.

Had I known in my mind's eye that something had happened last night and I had blotted it out, like some people who experience trauma and their brain goes into such a state of shock that they wipe their memory of it all? The only thing I did remember was the icy cold and the sulphur from the night before and it suddenly felt as though an icy hand had gripped my heart.

I sat and watched the news coverage on every station to see what was happening but there was nothing new from earlier. I had a call from the police who had asked me to come down the station and make a statement about the previous night, I had promised to go down tomorrow as I was still in shock about the deaths and they told me this would be ok.

All day I had sat and pondered on what could have happened, had whatever I had felt from that night materialised, no surely not. That was the stuff of creepy horror films, ghosts, ghouls and the like. However I still had the feeling that something had indeed come through, something, but what?

That night as I had sat, not watching, but staring at the television, I suddenly noticed they were showing an old Christopher Lee film 'The Devil Rides Out' and I made a note to watch this later, to see if it could give me any clues as to what might be happening. I switched the channel for the film on, made myself a coffee and sat down to wait for it to start. That is all I remember until the next morning, no dream, no nodding off watching the film.......nothing.

It is so frightening to lose time like that and even as I tell you, I don't remember what happened in my lost time. The memory of what happens totally eludes me. And that is why when I woke the next morning I was not prepared for what happened.

I woke in bed as I had the morning before but the smell of sulphur was in my nose and throat to the point of I threw up. Once I had showered and grabbed some coffee, I put on the news and settled down on the sofa with the sulphur smell still in my nostrils.

The news carried a story follow on from the night with Adrian's two friends and then showed a picture of a college guy, clean cut and quite handsome given a few more years, but then the camera flicked to a body covered in the same woods as the other two bodies had been found. My thought instantly turned to the reference I had made to him being handsome in a few years to the years would not happen for him and a tear slid down my cheek.

Why I was crying I don't know him but I did know for certain that all this had started to happen on Friday night and I would have to try and find out what was happening for everyone's sake. I picked up the phone and called Adrian but the phone just went to answer machine. Strange, it was still fairly early and he was not picking up. Maybe he was having a lie in, I suddenly thought.

I dressed and decided to go to the police station to make my statement early and get it over with and then I would pop round and see Adrian. The statement seemed to take an age after relentless questioning from a police officer and then it was all taken down and I signed dutifully at the bottom.

It was good to get out into the fresh air after being cooped up in that little stuffy room. The smell of sulphur still invading my nose and the feeling that the police officers did not believe a word she had told them. Maybe I was being stupid but I wondered if they knew I was keeping something back. Of course they knew they were not stupid. I had large chunks in my story which I could not account for, so I had either told them I was drunk or had gone to bed on my own to cover the missing parts. I stood outside for a short while just breathing the air into my lungs, in out, in out.

I felt less shaky now and made my way to my friend's house.

When I got there I was shocked to see Adrian's tearstained face. I asked him what was the matter and he blurted out that Mary had stormed out of here last night after an argument between the two of them about the Ouija night. She had not come back and she had not called him either to say she was safe. He had been out looking for her, called her friends, her mother to which Mary's mother had become hysterical with her daughter out there with a killer at large. Adrian had calmed her down by saying that she had just walked through the door, untruthfully.

I did not know what to say to comfort him I had known him since school days and had never seen him this way before. We sat and chatted for a while as I asked him if there was anywhere else she could have gone to, somewhere she had used to but stopped going to when they had married. He told me there was nowhere that he had thought of and the next logical step if she did not come back tonight would be to call the police. I asked him if he wanted me to stay with him and he told me that he would call me if he had any news. By the time I left there it was dark and there was once more a full moon. As I had done the other evening, I wrapped my coat tightly around me and made my way home.

I felt ***IT*** following me through the park just how it had on that first night. The wind whistling in the trees masking it's steps. I could not see it at first, just feel that it was there watching me. I walked a bit more briskly than I had, my heels thudding loudly on the pavement. I had told myself that I would not break into a run, but my mind was bordering on doing just that. The wind was whipping the trees into frenzy with the whistling sound ringing in my ears. I made it to the front door and sat in the dark listening to the noise until it became so high pitched that I had to cover my ears. Then it happened, I was looking through my eyes but it did not feel like it was me. I was stalking quietly through the woods, retracing my steps that I had taken earlier. Then I saw her, Mary walking towards the edge of the woods, heading home.

She turned quickly but I was much quicker and with a growling, snarling and a quick bite of the throat she was silenced. My reflection flickered in her now dead eyes and I was no longer me, I was some kind of demon, a wolf like you see in the old horror films. Then the recognition faded and below the glow of the full moon I savagely tore my victim apart, feeding hungrily.

The Night He Came Home

It is Christmas Eve and I am so tired, but on the other hand I am excited and want to stay awake for as long as possible to see if I could sneak a peek at Santa Claus. I am nine years old.

Mother has tucked me in and said her goodnight and left the room. I listened to see if I could hear Daddy come in from work and sure enough a few minutes later he did. I climbed out of bed and tiptoed to the landing to catch a glimpse of him as he blew me a kiss and I caught it as it travelled on the air up to me. Just as I knew he would he blew a kiss and once caught, he winked and I knew that was the signal to get straight back to bed. I don't know why my mother always put me to bed before Daddy came home. Maybe she just wanted some peace and quiet or maybe she knew that he would just want to spend as much time with me and ignore her as he did when the times arose to spend time with him.

Even though I was only nine, I knew there was a lot of tension between my mother and father; I just prayed every night that if they split up like my friend Becky's parents did, that I could live with my Daddy. But Becky had told me in her most annoying voice that the mother ALWAYS gets the child.

If this was going to be the case then I would defy my mother and make as much time as I could to spend with my Dad, even if she did not like it.

I crept slowly down the stairs and saw my father's legs outstretched and a paper in hand. Behind the paper she could see that he had his pipe lit as the smoke curled upwards into funny shapes.

Christmas carols played in the distance from the radio which was turned down low. I was so happy but something stopped me in my tracks and I crouched on the stairs just hidden in the shadows. My mother stood behind my father with the fire poker, she raised it high and stuck him hard on the top of the head.

Four sickeningly hard blows until eventually she could not pull the poker from his skull and he fell forward on to the rug, blood poured from the gaping wounds.

I couldn't bear to look but I do with one small fist held on my mouth to stop the cry that wants to escape from my mouth. Still sat in the shadows and totally out of view of my mother I watched her drag my father's body to the front door and once she has opened it she throws his body down the long flight of steps. From where I am sat on the stairs, I can see his body all broken and twisted at the bottom of the stairs, laid freezing in the snow. I then watch my mother clean everything in sight, no blood traces were left of what she had done. I swore then I would have my revenge on her for what she had done to my Daddy. Just as I was making my way back up the stairs I heard her on the phone, telling the police in a hysterical voice how her husband had slipped on the steps outside and she, hearing a thud outside, found him lying in a heap at the bottom of the steps, dead.

I could not believe what I was hearing, how could she have lied so convincingly, the next thing she was calling my name. From where I hid in the shadows I came running down to see what she wanted. If only she knew that I already knew the real story.

After my father had been buried, to which I was kept away from, I began to have dreams about him. In the dreams he came to me begging for my help to avenge his death. I would have only thought of these as being dreams but every time he appeared to me he was different. At first I did not know what the difference was but over time I could see his physical appearance was changing even though his loving heart towards me stayed.

One particular night, I felt as though I was half awake and half asleep. My father was there once more and when he asked me the same question with sadness in his eyes, I finally agreed. I told him that she had cashed his life insurance and just squandered it, rarely came home and left her on her own most of the time to fend for herself. This enraged my father even more and you could see the fury in his eyes, he wanted revenge but so much more also for the suffering she had caused both of us.

The night that my father came home was the most wonderful night of my life but not the same could be said for my mother. When she stumbled in through the front door drunk the night of his return, she thought she was going mad at first and tried to ignore him sat in his armchair. How she knew it was him I don't know, because by this time he was unrecognisable as my father. But she kept on averting her eyes every time they passed over his chair. As she walked passed with another drink, he grabbed her wrist suddenly and viciously and she tried to free herself from his grip. As she wrenched her wrist to get free, parts of his skin started to fall away from the bone but she struggled, screaming hysterically at him and eventually she just stood perfectly still like she was hypnotised. My father told me go to bed and sleep and things will be better in the morning and I did just as he said. I never heard any noises from downstairs after I shut my bedroom door. That night I slept soundly only once did I hear my father's voice which sounded different, more distant but I did feel him brush my hair with his hand softly.

The next morning I went downstairs to a silent household and called out to my mother who very rarely answered anyway, usually because she was in a drunken slumber. As I walked into the kitchen I noticed that the cellar door was open. I walked to the door and flicked the switch to see below. There she was my mother at the bottom of them, her back facing me but her head had been facing me. I knew that my father had given her the same manner of death she had given him and I smiled at the irony.

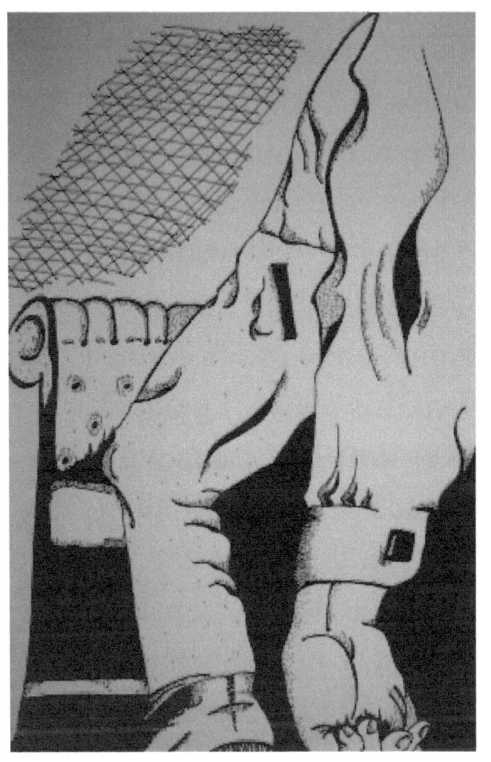

To Have and to Hold

I am stood in the church facing a man, who I loved and who I thought loved me saying my wedding vows in front of an expectant crowd of family and friends. It was a lovely wedding and the reception afterwards was very lavish. My husband is very wealthy but has not been given many attributes in the looks or charm department but I suppose there are lots of women who marry for money.....don't they??

I am the older bride as they say and I think the relief on my father's face on the day of the wedding said it all really.

The marriage starts off fine, a few little niggles from either side as time goes on but that is to be expected when you have never lived with anyone before.....is that not right???

But the troubles turned to violence and many times I had hidden myself away with the cuts and bruises of many vicious beatings. He would not let me work when we got married he believed that a woman's place was in the home, quite old fashioned were his views. I gradually over time lost touch with friends because of hiding away, my parents had been killed on their way back from a holiday in Spain and I had lost all the independence I had with my previous life.

The beatings became more and more violent until I was nursing broken bones. Trying to mend them the best I could but with that I ended up with an arm so badly put together that I could not lift anything with it and a leg which now had a bad limp and caused pain constantly.

He would not buy me painkillers so I had programmed my brain the best I could to overcome most of the pain I felt, he almost seemed to revel in the fact that I was in so much pain. He began to torture me when he forced himself on me during what he called his marriage rights. He would tie me up; tie things round my neck and pull hard on each end of the tie when he was pumping away inside of me. Just as I was about to pass out, each time, he would come inside of me. It seemed to turn him on and the more these things turned him on the more he would do them but he would worsen the pain and torture each time. A lot of the things he did were unspeakable and caused me irreparable damage that could not be fixed. He did not care, it was like he was an animal and I wondered while he slept if this is why he had never been married before.

When he was beating me once I had asked him why he did it and he told me to remember my wedding vows. To love, honour & OBEY, he would shout at me constantly. It was drilled into me and from then on as he beat me, scared me or broke my already fragile bones he would bellow those vows to me time and again. How could I forget what they were?

Time changed in my dream and came down to ten years gone by. I was now a broken woman, totally housebound and reliant on this monster I had married.

One day the dream changed to the sun on my face and the faint breeze blowing in my matted, grey hair. I was walking out in the sunshine for the first time in ten years.....out in the real world with real people. As people passed me standing in the front garden, they looked and then walked quickly away. One woman stood there screaming and people gathered to see what all the fuss was. I was oblivious to it all, just knew how good it was to feel the sun and the air, so fresh and clean.

The woman was still screaming when the police arrived. One of the police man told me to drop the knife and stand where I was. I looked down and suddenly thought......oh yes, the knife and I threw it to the ground.

But not the thing in my other hand that was mine, I deserved it. I remembered my marriage vows too but they were quite different. My vows came from the heart.

Yes I remembered the vows I had spoken and the heart I had ripped from my husband's chest as he slept was mine to keep.....to have and to hold from this day forward, in sickness and in health, till death do us part.

Life

Life, Love, Whatever......
What's it all about? I sit alone in this house, pondering on my thoughts of life, love, mysteries of the universe and so on and so on. Life passes by so quickly it is hard to keep up with all the changes.
Oh, I watch the news everyday on the television, it keeps me in touch with the outside world, but that is as close to the outside world I care to get. The changes out there, not always to my taste, but, hell, each to their own. Sigh....

Hey... I watched a funny film the other night on television. Let me see. That was it....The Meaning of Life with the Monty Python team. Funny, you have never seen anything like it. When they are all in heaven having a ball, when the fat man exploded (I particularly liked that, sick I know, but hey I love that kind of humour). The Mr Death scene when they have all died, well I nearly split my sides when Death told the American to shut up and made funny signals with its bony hands. Tears rolled down my face and thinking about it now brings a smile to my face.

Meaning of Life...what is the meaning of life? Why look at me? I am no philosopher, no disciple of god. I have been married and divorced, twice. Both times were not pleasant. I have gone through depression and stayed there for a long time, with the threat of suicide hanging over me for a considerable time. I still hang there now and again but the happy pills the doctor prescribes for me to take keep me, to a degree, balanced, not normal just balanced. So life, love, whatever, mean nothing to me.

If you talk to my doctor and all the counsellors he forced

me to see, they will tell you that this all probably started in my childhood. And to an extent I suppose it might, but the circumstances in years after that certainly did not help.
An unhappy childhood.
Beatings.
Etc, etc, etc. Blah, blah, blah!!!!!!

I don't care anymore I like my own little world here, with my films and my books. Yes, I forgot to mention about my books, I love them. I have so many there are not many more places to store them now. I often sit and read, music playing in the background. It's soothing and relaxing. Most people would not think that horror books are relaxing but they focus your mind, they keep you gripped and sometimes take you to places that are scary yet fascinating. What was the last book I read...let me see...Peter James, Host...yes that was it Host very interesting book, certainly kept me on the edge of my seat. I will definitely read more of his.

There you go then, that's probably my entire life put down on a couple of pages. Sad isn't it. Me, I like my life. It is peaceful, I can do what I want and even though I see what is happening in the outside world, I chose to stay away from it all.
Life and love, been there done that, not that bothered about the love. Think being dumped on all your life sees to that one....big time.

Life...I am not that bothered really if I live or die. Life is an existence, we are born and we die, circle of life, matter of fact. Some people go before others, some live long lives and some live a life like me, in my little cocoon of life, safe within my little room.

My little, padded room, where I was put after I murdered my mother. You see I had had

enough. My doomed relationships, my life of torment and ridicule and then my mother again leaves me. She promised me she would make an effort to try and build a relationship, but as always her promises to me meant nothing, never had and never would.
I saw her one day she walked past me and did not even look. I whirled round and hit her again and again and again. I can't remember how long it lasted for but her head was crushed, I know that. While I was doing it a red mist came before my eyes and I swore at that moment I was possessed. But you don't mention things like that here, not in the open, anyway. Keep it all inside, in your head where the world is safe.

I'm not mad in the way the white coat brigade would have you believe. I just lost the plot, as the young would say, had enough and just snapped. Mind finally reached a do not go any further border.
When they brought me here I did not remember much, but they have put me away forever, they taunt me with the fact when they want to upset me. They told me this as they chain me to the bed with leather straps and forced drugs into me. I don't mind the drugs, they make me feel mellow and I don't get the headaches when I am on them. Without them I don't remember much but know that I end up strapped a lot when I don't have my drugs. Funny, One Flew over the cuckoo's nest comes to mind. Wish we had a Red Indian here.....

I like to remember the things I used to have but can no longer have. So I make believe the world I want to be in, so life, love, whatever, I am happy and content in my head.

What Changed?

When did it start to go wrong? When did you stop loving me? Was it just now, had it been coming for a while?
I don't know
I look at the gashes across each wrist, the blood that is now welling up ready to spill over the edges. But I see past that. I see the look of hatred which was in your eyes when you spat the words at me: "You are just like her".
No, I was not like her.
I am labelled in the same category as her, his ex, the one who had tried to belittle & humiliate you. Who had pushed you to the brink of insanity he had labelled her and me the same.
Tears rolled down my cheeks as I remember the look in your eyes when he shouted that at me. After everything both of us had gone through in past lives and since we had been together. How could he?
I had stood by him no matter What had happened? A less supportive person would have fled long ago. Not that I ever would have, you see, for the first time in my life I felt that someone had made me happy and loved me and I could love them back with no conditions and no alterations to my personality. I had found the perfect man, so what had changed?
My head feels very woozy now. I look down at my wrists and see that the blood is trying to clot and I guess by now that I have lost a lot of blood.
Trying to think back on anything that would indicate when you had stopped loving me, I found that I could not think of anything but just what had happened that day. Was it that easy to fall out of love?
I had never been in love. My childhood and adult life had been a constant abuse chain, mental and physical. I had given up hope that anything

good would come my way, that love was never something that would enter my life, but that changed when I met you. Just a day out in the big city, I was not looking where I was going and we collided. We both knew there and then that we were meant to have met. We had been blissfully happy together and after three years of this blissful, love filled life I really thought this was it. Am I just stupid or gullible? Do I ask for it as one counsellor I had seen had told me on every session? There are people like you that end up with the same type of people over and over again, people who just take advantage of you and treat you how they want and you stick by them, try and make things work until you realise that things will not change.
Maybe she was right, but I can't help who I am. Even through all of it I have kept going. Yes, I have been depressed and yes, I have thought about ending it all, but I have never have gone through with it. This time however, I think tipped my mind too much.
The thought of you being so cruel when I had put my complete trust in you...... I had lain awake that night wanting to end it. Not wanting to be left on my own again (not that this really bothered me) but the thought of love never finding me, my future continuing to be as hard as my past. No, I could not live with that, my mind was in definite turmoil. You were sound asleep when I got up.
I sat down a scribbled a short letter about love, trust and life as I saw it. Then I took the knife from the kitchen, sat down and cut across my wrists. One after the other and very deep no return for me. I did not want to live in a life of continued torment I could not take that anymore.
I settled back in the chair and put the television on with no sound as to wake you and watched the flickering images

until the life, love and trust
that my body housed
completely drained from me.

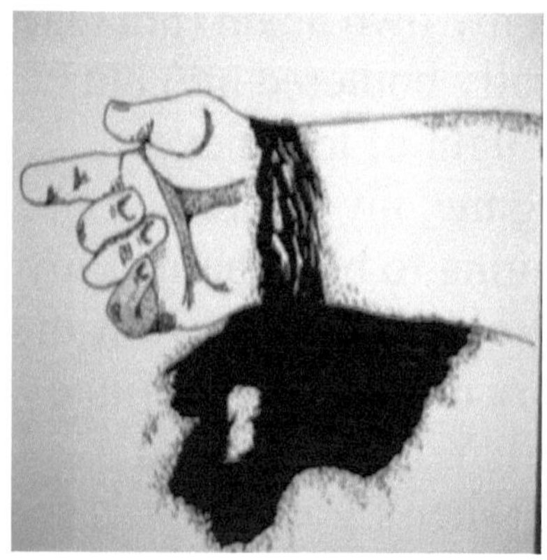

If Only Someone Had Listened

If they had listened to me this, the situation I am in, would never have happened. It's not my fault; it's theirs ......them out there.
I warned them. I told them many times that I would kill, but did they listen...... NO.
They gave me pills, sent me to a head doctor and then back for more pills. I told them I was possessed and they laughed.
'What are you possessed by?' they would ask with a smile on their fat sweaty faces.
I would look at each individually trying to determine if they were taking me seriously. Then it came out as blunt as I could make it.
'It is the scarecrow in the field at the back of my house'.
Their heads lowered and the sniggers began.
Why do you think that? They would ask.
Because it comes to me at night and tells me to do things, I reply, it tells me what I must do to bring it to life and all the voices he speaks with are all in my head, whirling around starting off softly and rising in pitch until it is little more than a screech......and then it goes.
The fat, sweaty faces converse with each other and then study me as though I am a beetle trapped under a glass. They scribble little notes and then they leave the room and I am alone.
The news that comes back to me is that I am totally mad and will be locked away. Not prison.....no, this will be a top notch security hospital. I am a danger to society, never to be let out.
I don't think they believed me about the scarecrow. Perhaps I should call them back into the room now as he is here with me.

Sat on the arm of the chair, opposite me.
He did not like the fact that I told, they might have believed me if I were not an eight year old boy and full of fantasies and ravings of a young child. You see......I did not mutilate my family, but I tried to warn them about the scarecrow, ever since he first came to me in my room. But they laughed just the same as the doctor's did. But he showed them, he came into the house one night and showed me just how powerful he was.

He started with my father, literally tore him limb from limb. My mother was next. I overheard the policemen talking when they came to the house, that my mother had been raped as well as mutilated, but looking at the scarecrow I could not believe he had the ability to do that. Then he had gone for my brother, a policeman was very sick when he came out of that room so I knew it was bad but they would not let me see. They just pushed me into the back of the car, drenched in blood. As we drove off I could see the scarecrow in the same place he always was, just hanging there as though nothing had happened.

The guards come back into the room and I expect them to see the scarecrow but they don't. As I try to tell them he is there they restrain me and place a strait jacket on me.
All the time, I can see the scarecrow and hear him laughing at me.
I just keep asking myself that if someone had listened to me in the first place.....none of this would have happened.

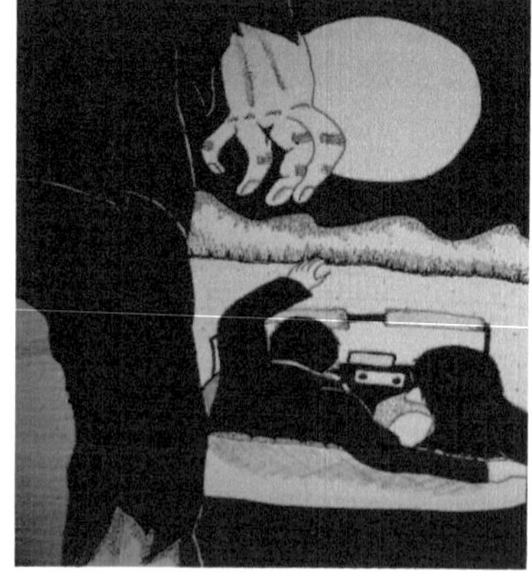

Greed

Josh knew something must have happened, somehow gone wrong and he was now feeling claustrophobic at the thought of being trapped in here. Josh screamed, a long high pitched and hysterical scream, but no one heard him. The plan certainly had not worked and it was he, now, who was living his own death sentence.

Josh and Tim Rodgers were devastated by life at the moment. Not only had their father died, but the house they thought would go to them, had been left instead to their stepmother providing that when she died, the house and the money would be left to them.

She had direct control over allowances, which she had drastically cut, claiming that they had been spoilt enough and now the twins were 25 years old they should stand up on their own two feet and not be dependent on hand outs constantly.

This did not go down well with the two brothers. Since they had been born, they had lived in luxury and did not want for anything. Their mother had died giving birth to them and their father spoilt them throughout life.

This had always been the case until he met and married Carol, their step mother. She had insisted he had not pampered them as much and make them realise that they could not stand on their own two feet if he kept spoiling them. But behind her back and against her wishes, he had carried on spoiling the twins. But a couple of weeks ago their father had suffered a massive heart attack and died on the way to the hospital and

now they were stuck with the stepmother from hell. She began by being tactful and leaving newspapers around the house, then they were always left on the jobs pages and now she had cut their allowances so they could barely survive. With this they decided that something had to be done about her.
They both knew that she also suffered from a bad heart due to an illness she had in childhood. She took pills on a regular basis for this and they had both thought about hiding the pills, but that would take to long for her to die, although as Tim had said he would have enjoyed seeing her suffer while she was dying. Josh thought his brother always had a sick, sadistic side to him. They finally decided that a terrible shock on a high enough level would stop her heart instantly only thing was what to do.
They had tried all the regular tricks, spider in the bath, snakes in the flower bed and Tim had even put maggots in the fridge. They had phoned the house number late at night firstly not making any noise and then threatening her but nothing was working so they came up with what they thought was the only way to ensure they got a result. They were both penniless and they needed the money to carry on the life style they had always lived. Josh had run up gambling debts in the thousands and Tim had been threatened with having his knee caps broken by some unsavoury characters and that would have just been the start of it.
They both knew that their step mother had doted on their father and knew that she visited the family crypt each day to place flowers near his coffin and they had both come to the conclusion that this was the only way to scare her. Frighten her into thinking that her husband had returned from the dead to let her know that

he was not happy how she was treating the twins.
They both set about their plans and went through it for a week until they had every last detail played out. Josh had agreed to be the one to slip into the coffin with his father. When the step mother came with the flowers he would hold his father up in the coffin with an arm pointing at her, what a shock that would be. Tim was to make sure that he slid the stone across enough to let him get a grip from the inside, and to make the voice seem as though it was his father's voice, they had even tested out their plan a couple of times and it worked perfectly.
The next afternoon Josh climbed into the coffin with his father placed on top of him. The smell was terrible but they both knew that it would all be worth it in the end. Tim hid in the shadows looking at his watch. He had not felt well the last couple of days, he felt clammy and his skin had taken on a grey pallor to it this morning, probably the flu he thought, I will get it sorted out when this is all over. When his watch showed 4.10 he walked over to the coffin and pushed on the stone coffin lid but he could not move it. He suddenly felt incredibly weak and tried to push it as hard as he could. Tim began to panic knowing that time and air were against them both then a sharp pain ripped across his chest and down his entire body. He dropped to his knees clutching his chest and hoped to will the pain away but it didn't and before that pain had gone another shot straight through his heart as though he had been electrocuted and he fell to the ground for the last time.
The step mother found Tim on the floor when she arrived at the crypt and called for help but it was all too late. She never saw Josh again and had no way to contact him about his brother's death. The police had told her that they had not found one clue to his

whereabouts. She knew that they were spoilt brats but she had loved them like they were her own children and she would miss having them around the house.

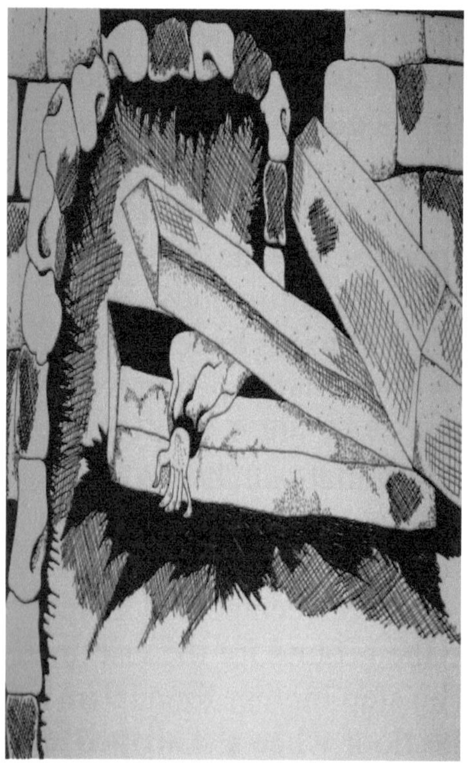

The Wishing Well

It was supposed to have been the best day of my life. All my wildest dreams were to be realised and acted upon but all I feel is sadness and despair.
I wished it that is the worst thing. I had that one wish, I took it and now I am paying the consequences.
I look down into the black hole that I had walked past all my life. It had been boarded up until we bought the house, my husband and I. We had opened it up and one fateful day I threw the penny in and made my wish.
I curse the day I ever did that and wish now, hope against hope, that the wish I am praying for now will come true. But I know it will not, how can it?
It's all too late.

The house and the garden had belonged to my grandparents when I was young. Wishing Well gardens my grandmother had called the place. When they had died, the house had become abandoned. My parents had tried to sell the place but everyone that had a look around it said there was something about the place, something uneasy and as a kid I could never understand it.
My grandparents had been wonderful people and I missed them so terribly even now. I remember the old wishing well my grandfather had built over an old well in the garden, he had told me the hole was not a place to be boarded over but a place to build upon and make it beautiful once more as it probably had been many years ago. I remember just sitting in the garden some summers and staring at the well and thinking about the old fairy tales my grandfather used to make up about the well and the little people who lived there. I hoped one day I would see one

of these little people but unfortunately that was not to be. When my grandparents had died, the well had been boarded over for safety reasons my parents had said.
I think I know now, as I stare into the murky depths, why they boarded it over.
When I was 21 I was given my inheritance from my grandfather's death, £2,000. This enabled me and my boyfriend David to marry. We had been together since we were 14 years old and we knew that one day we would have enough money saved to do it. I had already spoken to my parents about moving into my grand-parents home and they were ok with this but as it was still to be sold they would arrange for a small mortgage to be applied to the house for us as this money was to be for their retirement plans. We had everything we could have hoped for. We had love, favourable jobs and good prospects for the future. David and I refurbished the house and garden and made it our own. It was strange, I could feel the presence of my grand-parents in the house and garden, or maybe it was just memories of them here that made me think they were still about.
I remember the day well that I had made that stupid wish and when everything in my life started to go wrong.
It had been a particularly warm day and as I had the day off work, I decided to spend some time in the garden.
That was when I had stood over the wishing well, looked deep into the murky depths and thrown in my coin, wishing for wealth to come our way so that we could pay off the house and live very comfortably and maybe even retire early, David always worked so hard to make our life enjoyable and stress free from money worries.

Well two days after I made the wish, David was killed on his way home from work. The police had told me that eye witnesses had said he was swerving all over the road like he had been drinking. I knew for a fact that David did not drink and I told them this. They found that to be true and the verdict was accidental death. I was devastated by his death and nothing could console me. It was a week after his death that I found out he had insured his life for £1 million pounds. As I held the letter and cheque in my hands I had the strangest feeling go through my hands. Death had brought me what I had wished for but I would never be happy because of it.

Non Believer

Eric Jones was a paranormal activity researcher & writer but he was also a non believer of ghosts and the like. He thought for this reason being a writer of the paranormal he would be objective enough to know when someone was having him on. He was amazed by the power that paranormal activities had on people, he guessed it was their mind just wanting to believe than it actually being there. His latest research was to be carried out in a small village in Suffolk called Whitehaven. It was a typical small village heaped in history with its old looking houses all painted in bright colours and framed with wooden beams. It looked as though it had been the setting for an old film he had watched a few years ago called 'City of the Dead' and it had started Christopher Lee as a witch. He had often wished he could have found a village like that to work in, fog, evil and a place heaped in superstition and dread.
'Whitewood', he thought. Yes that was the name of the place. Looking around this village he thought he had found his Whitewood and he smiled triumphantly.
This place was supposed to have its fair share of superstition, witches and devils and when he first saw this place he knew he was onto a winner with the right atmosphere in which to write his book.
Coming to a stop, he placed his bags on the ground and pulled out a piece of paper from his pocket then began following the road around to the left until he stood in front of the place that was to be his working place for the duration of the next two weeks. He returned the paper back to his pocket and walked through the

doors of the White Swan Inn. After booking in, Eric was taken to his room, which was smaller than he anticipated, but it would do and for the rest of the night he busied himself with setting up his beloved typewriter and next to it placed his paper & pens. Sitting down at his desk, he got the first good look out of the window and found to his surprise he looked out onto the local church & cemetery, he loved it. The atmosphere and location were perfect.
Eric stretched over and picked up a blue file from his bed, opened it and emptied the cuttings out on his desk. The cuttings all related to goings on in this village and as he waded through them, he was amazed by the superstition and beliefs about goings on with the local church in particular. People now refused to go near or enter the church at all. He looked through his window and looked at the church in the distance wondering what had really happened there.
So many stories of things that he read were just whirling around in his head until he could no longer concentrate. He got up from the desk lay on the bed fully clothed and before long he had drifted into a dreamless sleep.
Eric woke the next morning to the sound of soft knocking on his door. He opened his eyes and his eyes were assaulted with brilliant sunshine and he closed them again for a moment only opening them again when he knew they would adjust to the light.
When the knocking came again he swung his legs off the bed and went to open the door. It was the landlady with a large tray of breakfast items. She was a short, overly plump woman and when she pushed past him into the room he let her but stood by the doorway waiting for her to put down the tray and leave. When she had left the room he looked down at the tray, placed all over his paperwork, with disgust and he picked up the tray and

placed it on the bedside table instead. With that done he grabbed the hip flask from his bag and took a long drink from it. He looked again at the fruit, muesli and coffee on the tray and took another swig from his hip flask and grimaced. This was something he had done to start the day for the last ten years and would probably do for the rest of his life.

Eric looked down at the cuttings on the desk and began to sift through them again. He was convinced that whatever was going on at the church he would find out, bring to an end and then people could go back once more to praying or whatever they did in those places. He had never entered one except to investigate praying would not do him any good. As he read he began to get the picture of what had happened in this village and placing all the cuttings in piles he found out that fifty out of the seventy cuttings mentioned strange goings on, ghostly lights, chanting and strange figures coming and going from the church. One resident said they had witnessed a ghostly congregation going into the church on the stroke of midnight, so terrified was he of the sighting he ran for his life, as the man had put it, as though the devil himself was chasing me.

Eric thought about the possibility that the guy had just come out of the pub and probably imagined it, but he was intrigued and was loathed to admit it to himself.

Eric made a mental not to see if he could track down the vicar and see what he had to say on the matter.

When he entered the church, he had the strangest feeling of doom. Most churches he had been in, even the ones that were supposed to have been haunted by monks and evil nuns, had been light and airy places with polished pews, the smell of must and the sparkle of stained glass windows.

This church however was different. It was like the sunshine had never reached into this place, the windows were dull and dreary looking with no stained glass for the sunlight to sparkle through. It smelt damp and mould grew near the altar, the pews were full of woodworm and the varnish was peeling off like the bark from a tree.
Eric shivered and mumbled to himself that he did not believe in evil.
Suddenly a voice rang out, "Maybe you should".
Startled Eric whirled round to put a face to the voice.
"I'm sorry to have frightened you. I am the vicar of this parish"
The man held out his hand and told Eric his name was Stefan Boyce. Eric could not help but stare at the vicar. Apart from the strangest accent he had ever heard, this man did not seem like a vicar, he had seen a few, but this man looked like his interpretation of the devil. His hair line was receding backwards at either temple to give him a pointed lock of hair on his fore head. It made you think of Christopher lee when he played Dracula. The vicars eyes sunk into their sockets deeply and were very dark rimmed, maybe from lack of sleep, Eric thought. His chin was very pointed and this made him look like an over stretched version of Jimmy Hill. It had looked as though God had given him the leftovers from everyone else's faces. When Eric saw the vicar's hands he was truly startled, they were like claws with long curled nails and Eric had visions of the vicar attacking him and ripping the beating heart from his chest in one swoop of those claws. No wonder no one wants to come here, thought Eric trying not to show his unease.
Eric told the vicar why he was here and the vicar gave a very sly grin and ushered him through to the vestry where refreshments were forthcoming. He poured

himself a drink and looked up when he realised the vicar was watching him intently it was an uncomfortable stare which seemed to build with the silence around them.

To break the silence, Eric related to the vicar the story of the ghostly church gathering made all the more sinister by the fact of this resident had been in the church porch way at the time.

The vicar nodded, “The story, unfortunately, has had bits and pieces added to it over time and now the locals refuse to come here”.

“Do you believe the stories?”

“Of course I do, I would not stand in the porch way late at night either”, the vicar replied with a sly grin.

Eric found out from the vicar that many had tried to stay in the porch way, some had run away and other’s had been found dead next morning. Eric had trouble taking all this in, he rubbed his eyes to try and shake the tiredness he felt and when he looked up the vicar had gone. Eric scoured the vestry and walked through to the church but could not find the vicar anywhere.

On his way out, he passed the porch way and studied it for a moment. After a while he moved away and made his way back to the inn but he would be back. Tonight he would come back for the stroke of twelve and he would dispel the rumours and gossip once and for all.

Eric listened and waited and just as he hoped by eleven thirty the village was as silent as the grave. He didn’t need any interfering but well meaning locals telling him stories of doom. Settling himself in the porch way the clock above him began to strike twelve. He listened and as the last stroke came and went along with it came silence once more. Nothing stirred, the night was deathly still and he was just about to give up and head back to the inn when he heard the gate creaking loudly, Looking up

he saw a crowd of people walking along the church path heading straight towards him but not really seeing him.
As the procession passed him he began to recognise some of the people he had spoken to in the village, people who had sworn that they never entered this church under any circumstances. As he watched them totally amazed, he realised one of them was........HIMSELF.
It suddenly felt as though his blood had run cold and his heart was going to explode. Blood pumped vigorously to his head causing a headache and with his hands squashed against both temples he ran as fast as he could, wanting only to get away from this place. He ran & ran as though his life would depend on it but he finally collapsed by a nearby gravestone panting heavily. He caught a glimpse of what was written on the stone, his eyes wide with terror and his heart beating way too fast, the inscription on the head stone was the last thing he saw.
"Here lies the body of the witch Stefan Boyce. Put to death for being a witch in the year of our lord 1536".

For the love of his son

Oh how he loved his son. Ever since the day that little bundle was handed to him in the hospital room. He had held him close while weeping for the death of his beloved wife and he had promised there and then that the little boy he held in his arms would want for nothing and would never come to any harm.
Looking down at this little wrinkled face, he placed a solemn oath that until the end of his days they would be inseparable. And he always kept his word.

The years rolled by and the little boy grew with so much love and attention placed upon his tiny shoulders that he doted on his father and wanted to spend every waking moment with him. When he was not in school they would go fishing, play football or just laze around in the garden just chatting about anything and everything. They had so much fun that the little boy preferred to spend time with his father more than he did with anyone else. However as the years rolled by so quickly the young boy found love with others. His father feeling so left out and alone begged him to stay home and be with him always. The young boy was torn. He loved his father very much but he had found a greater love in Annie. He had brought her home to meet his father but his father would just walk into another room and all he could hear was crying. He became embarrassed by what his father was becoming and told him so one night.
His father pleaded, begged but to no avail, his son had told him he was leaving and going to live with Annie. They would survive, they both had good jobs. His father could not take it and as his son turned to

leave, in a fit of anger, he picked up the fire iron stood again the mantelpiece and hit his son with it so hard it killed him with only one blow.
The father watched as his son hit the ground, stood hypnotised while he saw the blood grow and spread out on the carpet. He fell to the ground beside his son; taking his head on to his lap he began to cry and rock back & forth singing a lullaby of old.
Later that night when the last of the tears had been shed, he had fallen into a restless sleep on the living room floor. He dreamt his son was still alive and was waiting for him. His eyes sprang open as a strange noise invaded his ears. He tried to peer into the darkness and when his eyes adjusted, he saw the shadow stood in the doorway. He looked down beside him and realised his son was not there just a pool of congealed blood and the poker he had dropped earlier. He again looked towards the doorway and the shadow was now moving towards him slowly. As the glow from the moon caught the shadow he saw with relief this was his son. He was not dead, but he did look deathly pale or maybe that was just the moonlight shining upon his skin.
He crouched over to push himself up and that was when he felt the sharp crack on the back of his skull. Again and again it reigned down upon his head and as he rolled over onto his back he saw towering above him with the poker in his hand and just before that poker came down one more time he heard.
"Now you can have what you have always wanted father, for us to be together forever. Not in life but in death"

One Final Time

He woke up covered in sweat. The bedding was damp and clung to his skin like tight fitted clothing and the cold air in the room was bringing forth goose-bumps. He sat there, upright, for a few moments disorientated by the dream, no it was more than that. It was another premonition but somehow this was different he could feel it bearing down on him like a heavy weight that he knew he could not move until what he had dreamt had happened.

He had had many premonitions and it had all started when he had come home from that party and the drunk driver hit him and drove off. He had lain there by the curb with his cracked skull and suddenly it had happened he had seen what had happened to the driver even before the police told him. He had had dreams about people he knew and what they had coming in the future for them and it happened every single time. The most outstanding was his best mate winning the football pools and jetting off with his wife to foreign climes.

He grabbed the notepad off the bedside table, he had this because he had leant when the premonitions struck most were in a dream state and it was handy for writing things down while they are still fresh in his mind, and he began to scribble down dates that filled his head, places he thought he knew and he was in there so in some way he was part of this premonition this time round. Oh to win the lottery he thought, but he knew from the dream this was going to be nothing like that. He could see death, destruction, fire, screams, god how he wanted this image out of his mind. He always dreaded this happening.

When he first started to have the premonitions, he had read up on the subject and surprisingly lots of people had these but only a few had the death ones and unless there was something they tried to get others to help. He never wanted any of this but seeing as he was stuck with it he had learnt to do what he could with it.
The one main thing out of the whole of the dream was the whirring sound he could hear constantly and then a loud roar and could only assume that this was perhaps a gas explosion of some sort but perhaps things would become clearer as he found out more. That was one thing he did know that when the time came all would be revealed.
It had been three am when he had woken and now after dozing fitfully for most of the night it was 9am and he struggled out of bed and hopped in the shower. Drinking the coffee he had freshly brewed, he pondered on the nights notes on the scribbled pads. Firstly he had to find the building and that was a mighty task in Manchester. Most of the old buildings looked the same but if he could get up on top of one of the buildings and get a bird's eye view then he might stand a chance of recognising it. If he could not find it and get there in time all was lost, he had to try. The best place he had thought of was the top of the Arndale car park, that was high enough to give him the view he wanted and you could see quite a distance from there.
He quickly dressed and got into his car, which took an age to start and then died totally, the battery flooded. He did not like it, he knew the car played up constantly but he had never known it not to start and keep going. To him this was an omen, stay away. But he couldn't when he had seen the destruction that was about to happen, he couldn't sit back and do nothing. It was the

weekend before Christmas for god's sake the town would be heaving with people, could you imagine the devastation. It was unconceivable to even think of not doing something. He looked again at his scribbled notes which sat on the passenger seat. Picking them up and putting them safely in his pocket he locked the car and made his way to the train station. As he walked up the hill and then stood on the platform waiting for the train, he again pictured the building he was looking for when he got to Manchester. It was like an old factory type but it was hard to tell anything else from it as all he could conjure in his mind was the building in shadow. The dates he had were today's date and that was even more worrying, time was running out.

The train pulled in to the station and a shiver ran down his spine making him shiver violently. He hurried on the train as it started to rain heavily and finally settled down in a seat opposite a couple of young teenagers that seemed to have locked together with their mouths. He tried not to stare but it held his attention. They did not move that was the thing, they were just locked their lips to lips. All he could really see was two floppy fringes protruding from their hooded tops. He turned away and looked out of the window just as the train began to leave the station.

It was only a half an hour journey, and as they sped along he had a strange feeling that whatever was going to happen would be happening soon then he heard it the sound. A loud whirring sound and it got louder as it seemed to gather speed. Not only that but as he looked out of the window he could see it. The shadowed building there in the distance, he must have come past this on the train before and never even noticed it. Everyone was now looking around the train, some looking out of the windows to try and see what the noise was and that was when it happened, the explosion. So loud and then a bright orange and white blast burst forth from the end of the train carriage. As the smoke cleared I could just make out that the end of the train carriage had disappeared. People were screaming, covered in blood and some walking blindly holding on to seats to get to the other end of the carriage and then there was another blast and all turned black.

I came to for a short time to see that I was now lay in a field with a couple of chairs covering me and I tried to sit myself up. I couldn't move it felt as though I had just my head and that was hurting incredibly. There was no sensation anywhere else. I tilted my head to the side and the last thing I saw before I died was bodies scattered everywhere not sure if it was from the train carriages or the plane that had landed on top of the train. In the distance was the shadowy building shown in my last premonition.

One Time to Many

He was a pro. A skilled burglar, an old hat at this so where was he going wrong. He had never been caught, never felt the law grabbing his collar like his mates had, but things had changed since he had been away. The thing was he had been in a coma for six years, no one knew who he was, never kept any identification on him in case he was nabbed. When he had finally come to he had been told by the nurses that he had fallen from the roof of a building and it had been the fall that had put him in the coma. The police had wanted to ask him why he was up on the roof in the first place but he could not remember. Apart from knowing what he did for a living he did not even know his own name, where he lived. No identification you see.

He did not know if he was married, single, had kids. He could only assume that either he had been a complete bastard to his wife and she was glad he had disappeared, or that he was indeed young free and single. Whatever it was married or single, he was now on his own and with only the skills he could remember from his past able to feed himself. But he did wonder to himself, why was it only his skills at being a burglar that he did remember. Why was he in this situation now? Surrounded and caged, one thing that always scared him the most in life and he supposed the main reason he had avoided being locked up. He could never have stood going to prison and being locked up for years. But this.......this was much worse. Panic set in as he lay there waiting for death to claim him.

When he had left the hospital earlier that day, he started to make his way to the homeless shelter they had given him the

address for at least he would have a bed for the night and somewhere to think.
When he arrived at the shelter, there were a lot of smelly and dirty looking individuals who seemed fascinated by his presence but he just tried to steer clear from them all and when it got too much for him he took himself off into the streets for a walk. Walking around he made a mental note where he was going as this place was totally new to him. If this had been his hometown as he had been told then he could not remember this place either.
Tall buildings lined the streets as he walked, some with lights on, some in total darkness, but one thing he kept noticing was the alarms on the outside of the shops. My god how do you get past those without them giving you away he had thought to himself. He stood looking at one for a moment and had a memory of these making their way into the world and how good they were at catching a burglar out without even making a noise in the shop. But they were certainly going off in some local police station somewhere. Just as you stepped out the door, arms laden with goods, they were waiting. He had seen some of his mates go that way, he suddenly remembered. He smiled and shook his head as he walked off. He would be better finding some little place somewhere, full of treasure that he could be in and out of in a second. No alarms, no mess and no fuss.
He pulled his collar up tight around his neck. He hadn't felt the cold until just now and he was freezing. He was just thinking of making his way back when there it was, a little junk shop tucked down a small alley and way out of view of anyone's gazing eyes, especially copper's, he thought.
He ambled down the alley and stood opposite lighting a cigarette just looking out of

the corner of his eye. No alarm was to be seen. It also looked as though the bolts on the door would be easy enough to force and one single old fashioned brass handle to turn. He crept towards the shop window just keeping an eye on the street and one eye on the window so that if someone walked past then they would think he was just browsing. On the window read 'Treasure's Galore the store you will never want to leave'.

When he felt the time was right, he pushed on the door as hard as he could to force the lock. But it was not even locked and just as the door pushed open a little door bell chimed and he quickly put his hand up to stop the tinkling noise. He held himself very still for a moment making sure that there were no lights coming on or anyone that would disturb him. He was safe.

He had a bit of light that came into the shop via a street lamp and that helped him move around. Blimey, he thought, this is a junk shop to beat all junk shops. The place was crammed with weird looking stuff. There was a stuffed bear just stood there in one corner trying to look fierce but the mangy look it had to the fur made it look as though it had seen better days. A fish stuffed in a glass tank with a little plaque which he could not quite read attached to the front left hand corner. Then there were masks that looked as though they had come from foreign climes, swords on the walls and old fashioned shot guns. He then spotted what he had come for it was right up the front a big glass showcase that had all antique jewellery in it. There were gold watches, rings, bracelets, brooches, you name it and that was what he had in front of him. He tenderly played with the lock on the sliding door and eased it gently careful not to make any noise.

He began to fill his pockets until they weighed him down

and he went on a hunt for a more suitable bag to carry the goods in. Right at the front of the shop were some old coal sacks and he shook one of those open and began to load in the jewellery. He thought of the old swag bags and chuckled to himself.
Just as he had the last handful in his fist ready to thrown into the coal sack, a light switch clicked and light flooded the back of the shop. The sudden flash of light startled him and he dropped the handful of jewellery and the coal sack and ducked down behind the counter, almost falling onto the glass counter.
A shadow fell over him and he eased himself up on his elbow to be greeted with the elderly face of a man. The face looked more like a skeleton with the skin stretched tight over it and the mouth was stretched as though in a permanent grimace. He wore a flat cap and a pair of trousers held up with braces resting over his bony frame which was partly covered with a string vest.
“So what do we have here?” said the old man in a hoarse sounding voice.
He looked up into the eyes of the old man and there was something not right. The old man’s eyes shone with a burning fire of red and seemed to burn into his very soul, he could not shake the feeling of doom and he should not have entered this place, he should have just stayed away. But that was too late now. His mind was in a whirl of panic and he pushed himself up quickly and made for the door. He suddenly stood very still, there was no door, no shop window that he had looked into just a short while ago, where had it gone?
Panic stricken he turned round quickly and saw the old man exactly where he was when he had hovered over him. He turned his head quickly from left to right, searching for anything that he could use to get himself out of here. The

door must be here somewhere, he thought. But there was nothing.
He had the strangest feeling of not only being watched by the old man but also by others. Eyes following his every move and revelling in his panic. Maybe it was the way the bear looked suddenly vibrant in the light it's coat now with a glossy shine to it or the fish in the tank, was it watching him too. That really panicked him. "Have to get out of here", he muttered to himself.
He saw on the wall near to him the old shotguns and grabbed one off the wall and below them on a shelf were some cartridges which he began to load the guns with. One gun under his arm loaded and the other pointing at the old man he began to slowly edge towards the counter once more with a view to getting out the back. The old man stayed where he was only staring at the gun barrel being pointed at him, with the strangest of smiles on his face.
It was then that he heard the low growl and thinking it was a dog that belonged to the old man, he tilted the gun to the floor as he edged closer to the old man. He could not see a dog anywhere but the growl was getting louder and closer but still there was no sign of a dog. The old man had not moved from his spot and the glow from the light behind him made him look like a dark shadow but his eyes still glowed red. As he was watching the old man's eyes, he suddenly felt the sharp grabbing of his skin and pulling from behind then hot breath was upon him as he fell fatally wounded to the ground. His back was burning.
He could hear the panting and felt the hot breath on the back of his neck and something else. He tried to roll himself over onto his back as best he could even though he did not really want to see what was there. Moving gave tremendous pain so he just pushed with one arm with as

much strength as he could muster and flopped on to his back. A searing pain shot up his back and down his legs, he screamed loudly and it felt like a long time before he stopped gritting his teeth and opened his eyes.
And there it was, what he had feared would be behind him, the mangy bear he had seen previously. It now had a gleam to its coat that made the fur shine. Its eyes glistened like glowing red hot embers just like the old man's eyes and they glared at him with hatred. Its hot breath fell on his face as it panted and the blood dripping from its open jaws he knew was his blood. It hovered over him so close to his face that blood splashed into his eyes from the blood red teeth. Staring into those shining red eyes he did not know what to do but he had to do something. Out of the corner of his eye he could see the old man next to the bear stroking its fur as though it were a dog and telling it to hold back. The bear looked up at the old man and that was when he shot his hand out to the gun laying next to him and fired.
When the smoke finally settled he realised that it had done nothing and at first he thought either the gun was that old and could not fire or the bullet casings were empty.
But then the old man looked at him and said, "Silly boy. You can't kill us. We are already dead. Have you not looked around you and see that all my treasures have now come to life?"
He looked around him and saw that everything that once stood in the dark and dusty corners had now come closer and were staring down at him. Scarecrows, mannequins, and a tailors dummy with no head he felt very claustrophobic. The pain in his back increased and he knew the amount of blood that he was losing would mean he would be dead soon. He tried to talk to the old man but blood shot past his

lips and dribbled down his chin.
The old man looked at him and said “I know what you are thinking.....how? We don’t need any alarms or new types of gadgets. We all of us have a story in history to tell in this shop but not one of us in here now will be missed and not one of us here has a place in mankind. I collected my treasures one by one. Rejects that people had thrown out and not wanted, old fashioned pieces that people tire of when they have had their pleasures from it. Or just things that people have killed for the hell of it like my bear here. In this little shop we all have a purpose in life, to protect each other. You are one of those rejects from life you don’t know yourself no-one knows you and you will never be missed. But now you have a family and our family will grow over time”.
With that all the figures that crowding in on him moved back into the shadows, the old man disappeared into the back room and turned off the light and the last thing that he saw before death took him was the mangy old bear with the fur all mattered and torn return to its rightful place.
Protecting its family.

www.ingramcontent.com/pod-product-compliance
Ingram Content Group UK Ltd.
Pitfield, Milton Keynes, MK11 3LW, UK
UKHW041837200726
13854UKWH00003BA/1177